COVENTRY LIBRARIES

Please return this book on or before
the last date stamped below.

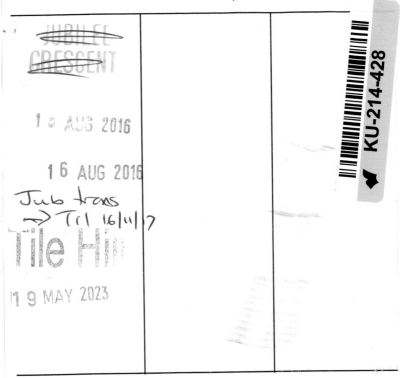
To renew this book take it to any of
the City Libraries before
the date due for return

Coventry City Council

REA

ReadZone

www.ReadZ(

© in this edition 2016 ReadZone Books Limited

This print edition published in cooperation with Fiction Express, who first published this title in weekly instalments as an interactive e-book.

FICTI●N
EXPRESS

Fiction Express
First Floor Office, 2 College Street,
Ludlow, Shropshire SY8 1AN
www.fictionexpress.co.uk

Find out more about Fiction Express on pages 89–90.

Design: Laura Durman & Keith Williams
Cover Image: Hunt Emerson

ISBN 978-1-78322-583-5

Printed in Malta by Melita Press.

SNAFFLES
AND THE MOONFISH MYSTERY

CAVAN SCOTT

What do other readers think?

Here are some comments left on the Fiction Express blog about this book:

"I think the book is amazing. I totally loved the ending."
ED, Crawley

"I loved the fishy jokes. Really good story"
Emma K, Emsworth

"My class are loving the new novel. I dressed up as Snaffles for World Book Day and the class guessed right away who I was. Well done. Another great Snaffles story"
Miss Harley, Moray Primary, Falkirk

"I think it was like a James Bond film. It had a lot of action in it."
Andrew, Emsworth

"I don't think it was good, it was amazing!!! I loved the ending with all those funny jokes."
Magena, Crawley

Contents

For Chloe and Connie

Chapter 1

Teatime Terror!

Are you looking forward to eating your tea?

I bet you are. Perhaps you're already feeling peckish. Your stomach rumbling. Your mouth watering. Thoughts of all that yummy food.

Me too – but before you get *too* hungry, let me ask you another question.

Has your tea ever tried to eat *you*?

No? Well, that very thing has happened to Snaffles the Cat Burglar.

You know who I'm talking about,

don't you? Snaffles the Cat Burglar is officially the world's greatest thief. There's nothing this cat can't nick, from precious jewels to priceless paintings.

Why, only last Sunday he broke into the Louvre museum in Paris and made off with the *Mona Lisa*.

And the day before that, he raided the gold reserves of Fort Knox in America. Stole every single bar of the shiny stuff.

Yesterday, he even managed to get into Buckingham Palace and pinch the Queen's favourite diamond-encrusted toilet.

There isn't a lock Snaffles can't pick, a burglar alarm he can't beat or a security system he can't scramble.

He really is the best of the best.

Or maybe that should be the best of the worst, because, as your teacher will tell you, crime does not pay. Unless, of course, your teacher is also a criminal mastermind. You never know. Take a long hard look the next time you see them. Do they look shifty to you? If so, yes, you are probably being taught by a world-class criminal. Congratulations. But even then, they still won't be half as good as Snaffles.

Anyway, while crime may not pay, it certainly makes you hungry. Snaffles was starving. He'd just got back to his top-secret lair and was famished. Luckily, Bonehead was in Snaffles' top-secret kitchen. Unfortunately, Bonehead is possibly the world's worst cook.

"How long until tea's ready, Bonehead old bean?" Snaffles called out.

"Almost there, boss," came the reply. "I'm just warming the custard."

"Custard?" A frown crossed Snaffles' furry face. "I thought we were having grilled trout?"

"We are," Bonehead shouted back. "The custard's for the mashed potatoes."

See what I mean? Bonehead is such a bad cook that he even burns ice cream. It's really not surprising. Bonehead the bulldog is Snaffles' trusty sidekick, and while the dotty dog has a big heart, it's fair to say that he also has an exceptionally small brain.

Snaffles was just wishing that he'd ordered in pizza, when the door to his top-secret dining room crashed open and Bonehead bumbled in. He was holding a large silver platter, complete with a lid.

"Sorry boss," he said, looking worried. "You'll have to make do without custard."

Snaffles let out a sigh of relief. "Thank heavens for that."

"I couldn't get it out of the kettle," Bonehead explained.

Snaffles couldn't care less about a kettle full of thick, gloopy custard. The smell coming from the silver platter was absolutely mouth-watering. He could already imagine the tasty trout, cooked to perfection beneath the polished lid.

Bonehead slammed the platter onto the dining table, only smashing three plates and a wine glass, which was a personal record. He cleared his throat and announced in his grandest voice: "Tea is served, innit!"

Snaffles snatched up his knife and fork, and licked his lips as Bonehead lifted the platter's lid.

And that's when it happened. That's when Snaffles' tea decided to eat him.

Before you could say 'pass the tartar sauce' the troublesome trout leapt from the silver plate, opened its surprisingly wide jaws and closed them again around Snaffles' head.

"Get it off me!" the cat cried, hopping around the top-secret dining room. Unfortunately, due to the fact that he had a large fish on his head, the command sounded more like "Mff ff mff mf!" to Bonehead.

The baffled bulldog just looked a bit cross. "Boss, don't you know it's rude to play with your food?"

It was only when he noticed the fish's glowing red eyes that he realized something was wrong. "Boss," he spluttered. "That fish is trying to eat you!"

"You think?" Snaffles screamed back, prising the trout's mouth apart to be heard.

"Hang on," shouted Bonehead, disappearing into the kitchen. "I have a plan!"

He returned two seconds later and – CLANG!

"Owww!" yelled Snaffles. "What was that? It felt as if someone just hit me on the head with a frying pan!"

"Yeah, that was me," grinned Bonehead, still holding the rather large kitchen implement. "I was trying to knock the fish off you! Hang on, I'll try again!"

To Snaffles' despair, he raised the frying pan once more....

Chapter 2

Something Fishy Going On

Bonehead swung the frying pan back, as if he was a Wimbledon champion about to take the winning serve.

"Wait!" Snaffles screeched, scrabbling around blindly on the dining table. Eventually, he found what he was looking for, his ginger paw closing around a large peppershaker that he'd 'borrowed' from the Ritz restaurant a few years before.

Before Bonehead could take another swing, Snaffles flicked open the shaker and threw the contents all over the fish.

As soon as the pepper hit the trout's gills, the fish began to shake, before letting out the biggest sneeze you've ever heard.

The fish shot from Snaffles' head like a cork from a bottle, bounced off the ceiling and flopped back down onto the table. It floundered around for a second, before its murderous red eyes fixed once again on the recently chewed cat burglar. Snarling menacingly, the terrifying trout sprang towards Snaffles, still aiming for the freaked-out feline's face.

"Watch out," said Bonehead trying to hit the flying fish with the frying pan.

"Ouch!" said Snaffles, as his stupid sidekick clonked him on the head instead.

"Aaaaaargh!" screamed the fish as it flew out of the top-secret dining room's top-secret window and landed with a plop in the River Thames outside.

"So," said Bonehead, as he watched the fish get washed away. "Fancy a sandwich instead, boss?"

"Fancy a sandwich?" Snaffles repeated, not quite believing what he was hearing. "My meal just tried to bite my head off, you pea-brained pup! Something extremely odd is going on!"

"You're telling me," agreed Bonehead. "I've got a dent in my favourite frying pan. How did that happen?"

Ignoring Bonehead and still rubbing the frying-pan-shaped lump on the back of his head, Snaffles plucked a remote control from a pouch in his belt. With the click of a button, a large television screen whirred down from

the ceiling and blazed into life. Snaffles
flicked through the channels until he
found the news.

"*Something extremely odd is going on,*"
the serious-looking newsreader said.
"*All over the world, fish are attacking
innocent people.*"

Images flashed across the screen. A
fisherman fighting off a trio of troublesome
tuna with his fishing rod. Customers in
a fish and chip shop getting battered by
a crabby cod. A TV chef being poked in
the eye by a ferocious fish finger.

And what's more, each and every fish
had glowing red eyes. Well, except for
the fish fingers, obviously. Although
their breadcrumbs seemed to shine in a
suspiciously sinister manner beneath
the studio lights.

Snaffles paused the image. "It's almost as if someone somewhere is controlling them all, from the smallest sprat to the largest shark!"

"But who could do such a thing?" asked Bonehead, scratching the back of his neck – a sure sign that the bulldog was confused. In case you didn't know, Bonehead scratched his neck a lot!

"*That's exactly what we want you to find out!*" a voice boomed from the television screen. The face of an elderly man with a humongous moustache had replaced the news report.

"Admiral Theodore Grandchops," Snaffles exclaimed. "Head of the Ministry of Secret Shenanigans, spymaster supreme and winner of the bushiest facial hair contest seven years running!"

"*I hate to say it, Snaffles, but we need your help… again,*" Grandchops begrudgingly admitted. The cat burglar had worked with the Ministry of Secret Shenanigans before, helping them defeat his arch-nemesis, Professor Wicked-Whiskers, and a maniacal mouse named Gorgonzola. Neither thief nor spymaster particularly liked each other, but at times of great peril the two rivals would pool their resources to save the day.

Grandchops pointed a podgy finger at Snaffles from the screen. "*The fate of the entire planet is in your paws!*"

* * *

Minutes later, Snaffles was speeding down the Thames in his top-secret speedboat, Bonehead's scarf blowing in the breeze.

"I wish you'd let me make a sandwich before we left," Bonehead grumbled, rubbing his empty tummy. "We still haven't had any tea!"

"No time for tea, old boy," Snaffles said. "We need to find out who is controlling the world's fish, and fast!"

"But where are we going?" Bonehead asked, checking beneath his woolly hat just in case he'd hidden a cream cake under there in case of emergencies. Instead, he just found a note to remind himself to hide a cream cake in his hat in case of emergencies.

"To find some fish, of course," Snaffles said with a smile. "The London Aquarium is just around this bend in the river!"

Bonehead was about to ask if the London Aquarium had a café when something hard smacked against the bottom of the boat. It flipped into the air, throwing Snaffles and Bonehead into the churning river. As they dropped beneath the surface, Snaffles found himself staring into a pair of glowing red eyes.

Something was in the water with them!

Chapter 3

A Shocking Encounter

Don't panic, Snaffles thought as the red eyes rushed towards them. That was easier said than done. It was so dark in the water that he could barely tell which way was up or down. Of course, most cats wouldn't even want to be this near water, but as you know, Snaffles isn't just any ordinary cat!

Near him, Bonehead floundered around, probably trying to remember if he could swim. The mutt's memory wasn't great at the best of times. He usually had trouble remembering his own name. He'd once gone an entire week thinking he was called Penelope!

But now the dippy dog was in trouble. Those ferocious eyes were heading straight for him, accompanied by what looked worryingly like a row of needle-sharp teeth!

Snaffles kicked his legs, propelling himself towards Bonehead. He tucked a paw beneath three of the canine's chins and swam towards what he hoped was the surface.

As they struggled up, Snaffle's tail brushed against something hard and slimy. His fur immediately stood on end as electricity crackled up his spine.

"Yeow!" Snaffles cried as they broke the surface. "That hurt!"

"Boss," Bonehead spluttered. "Do you think that was one of those mind-controlled fishies? It didn't look very friendly!"

"It's worse that that, old thing," Snaffles said, peering into the murky depths. For a second, a long, twisting body was illuminated in the darkness. "It's an electric cel – and it's coming back. Look out!"

The two friends only just managed to throw themselves out of the way as the foul fish burst out of the water, electricity crackling along its scaly skin. The monster's massive jaws snapped together and it crashed back down into the river.

"Oi," Bonehead barked after the creature, "if anyone is going to do any biting around here, it's me!"

Before Snaffles could stop the brave-if-brainless bulldog, Bonehead clamped his teeth around the eel's fast-disappearing tail. Bonehead loved biting things – it was one of his favourite pastimes, along with chasing parked cars and sniffing lampposts. However, biting an electric eel was probably not the brightest thing Bonehead had ever done – and that was really saying something!

ZAAAAAAAAAAP!

Electricity surged through the bulldog's body and, for a moment, Snaffles could see Bonehead's skeleton as if he was a living X-ray!

Angrily, the eel flicked its tail, sending Bonehead flying through the air to land in a quivering heap on the bank of the river.

"That does it!" hissed Snaffles, his mind made up. "It's time to give this slippery customer the, er, slip!"

Diving back beneath the water, Snaffles looked around for their aquatic attacker.

There you are, he thought, spotting the creature sparking near the riverbed. *Recharging your batteries, eh? Well, perhaps it's time you got a shock for once!*

Spinning his tail around like a propeller, Snaffles rocketed down through the freezing-cold water. Noticing the plummeting pussycat, the eel started swimming up to meet him. They bolted towards each other, the eel's mouth yawning open.

Holding his nerve as well as his breath, Snaffles waited until the last possible minute and swerved to the side. The eel streaked past him, twisting around as it realized it had overshot its prey. Snaffles pulled up, the eel snapping at his heels. His tail whizzing, the cat burglar darted this way and that. The eel matched his every turn – but Snaffles' plan was working! With every twist, the fearsome fish tangled. Its muscular body coiled around and around and around, until it had tied itself into a tight knot.

Unable to move, the eel made one last frantic lunge for Snaffles. The cat burglar was almost out of breath, but dodged the ferocious jaws. Instead, the eel's teeth sank deep into its own tail.

CRACKLE! SPARK! FIZZ!

With electricity flowing up and down its shuddering body, the eel sank to the bottom of the river.

Snaffles wasn't out of danger just yet. His lungs empty, he couldn't help but gasp. As he did so, foul-tasting water rushed into his mouth. The cat burglar thrashed helplessly about in the gloom.

Just then a strong paw grabbed the scruff of his neck. His body limp, Snaffles was dragged back up to the surface, his rescuer doggy-paddling like crazy! One minute, Snaffles was in the water and the next he was on the riverside, gratefully gasping lungful after lungful of wonderful air.

"Bonehead!" Snaffles wheezed as the delighted dog's face loomed over him. "I thought you were electrocuted?"

"It'll take more that a little fishy to finish me off," the bulldog grinned, "or my name's not Penelope."

Snaffles didn't bother to argue. They were running out of time. Pulling his aching body up from the pavement, he ran across to the large glass doors of the London Aquarium.

"They're locked," Bonehead said, rattling the handle.

"Not to me," Snaffles said, popping claws that were tougher than any diamond. With a noise like an entire packet of chalk scraping across a blackboard, Snaffles cut a perfectly round circle in the glass and slid his arm through the hole. A moment later, he'd thrown the latch and they were in.

"This way," Snaffles said, rushing into the tourist attraction's main hall, only to come skidding to a halt a second later. Even Bonehead managed to stop himself barging into his boss's back when he saw what awaited them.

Chapter 4

Aquarium Antics

The walls of the London Aquarium were lined with hundreds of enormous tanks containing thousands of fish.

Thousands of fish that were glaring at them with thousands of glowing red eyes!

If this wasn't enough, the fish started shouting at once, a single deep voice booming from all of their tiny fishy mouths.

"FOOLS," it bellowed. "YOU DARE TO DEFY THE MIGHT

OF THE GREAT MOONFISH?"

"Who?" Snaffles asked, raising a mocking eyebrow. "Sorry, old chap, but I've never heard of you!"

"BUT I HAVE HEARD OF YOU, *SNIFFLES* THE CAT *BUNGLER*! PREPARE TO FALL QUAKING BEFORE MY FINS!"

"Oh yeah," said Bonehead. "You and who's army, eh?"

In response to Bonehead's question, every fish in every tank swam back a few paces, their tails thrashing.

Snaffles' eyes narrowed. "I don't like the look of this, Bonehead, old bean." The fish swam back a little further.

Bonehead scratched the back of his neck. "It looks as if they're retreating. Maybe they're just scared of you, boss?"

As one, the fish smiled. Have you ever seen a fish smile? It's one of the creepiest things in the whole wide world, with or without glowing red eyes!

"CHARGE!" the voice yelled and the fish darted forward, ramming the side of their tanks as one.

"They don't look too scared to me," Snaffles admitted, as cracks started spider-webbing across the glass. Water immediately began to seep through the ever-widening gaps, the tanks bulging, before:

CRAAAAASH!

Each and every tank in the aquarium burst at the same time, water and fish flooding into the room.

"Run!" Snaffles yelled, but it was too late. A wave of water gushed over them, fish swarming to attack from every angle. As Bonehead battled a bevy of Bluefin tuna, a shoal of shad snapped angrily at Snaffles' fur, while a sticky starfish slapped itself over the cat burglar's face.

For the second time that evening, Snaffles couldn't breathe. He rolled about in the water, trying to free himself of the five-legged freak. Suddenly, something hooked on to his collar and yanked him up. Was it Bonehead, coming to the rescue once again?

With a plop, the starfish let go. Tossing it away, Snaffles glanced around to see a large moustachioed man holding a large fishing rod!

"Grandchops!" Snaffles exclaimed as he was pulled into a brightly coloured dinghy beside Bonehead. "What is the head of the Ministry of Secret Shenanigans doing here?"

"No time to explain," Grandchops blustered, unhooking the line from Snaffles' collar and gunning the dinghy's engine. The small boat sped out of the aquarium, riding the cascading tank-water back into the Thames. "While you were distracting our mystery marine mastermind, the Ministry's boffins traced his mind-control beam! We've found his base!"

"Then, where is it?" Bonehead asked, struggling to shake loose a lobster that had attached itself to his nose.

"Up there," Grandchops said, pointing into the night sky.

"The moon?" Bonehead gasped, finally dislodging the crafty crustacean.

"Of course," Snaffles said. "*Moon*fish! That's what he called himself, remember?"

Grandchops nodded gravely. "The fishy fiend is attacking Earth from space, which is why we're heading to the Ministry's top secret launch pad!"

"Its *what*?" Snaffles asked, fearing the worst.

Admiral Grandchops flashed a wicked grin. "Ever fancied becoming an astronaut, Snaffles?"

Chapter 5

Take Off!

Half an hour later, Snaffles and Bonehead were strapped into two large, bulky spacesuits and sitting behind the controls of the Ministry of Secret Shenanigans' very own rocket ship. Neither looked particularly happy about it!

"Is this a good time to mention that I don't like heights?" whimpered Bonehead from the co-pilot's seat, staring up towards the stars.

Grandchops' voice came over the radio. "There's nothing to worry about.

This is going to be a real blast!"

"That's what I'm worried about," admitted Snaffles, as he shifted uncomfortably in his suit. "How many times have you launched this thing?"

"Never before!" Grandchops said. "It's her maiden voyage, but we're absolutely, completely and utterly convinced that she won't blow up... probably!"

"Whaaaaat?" Snaffles cried out – but the countdown to launch had already begun.... Admiral Grandchops' voice boomed over the rocket's loudspeakers, fighting to be heard above the roar of the engines.

"*10. 9. 8. 7. 6...*"

The entire spaceship was shaking now. Snaffles' teeth chattered together as his chair vibrated violently.

"… 5. 4. 3. 2. 1!"

This was it. The rocket strained against its scaffolding on the launch pad, desperate to fling itself into space.

"*Blast-off!*"

The rocket shot into the sky, crushing g-forces pushing Snaffles back into his seat. It was like nothing he'd ever experienced before.

Not that it seemed to be worrying Bonehead, who had dozed off in his comfy chair, drool dribbling from the side of his mouth. Seriously, that dog could sleep through *anything*!

Snaffles wished he could curl up and get a cat-nap. All he could hear were the engines, drowning everything else out – even Bonehead's snoring!

Snaffles felt as if his eardrums were

going to burst at any second. He screwed up his eyes, curled his paws into fists and waited for it all to be over.

Then, all of a sudden, everything went quiet. The engines cut out and for a moment Snaffles thought that they were about to spiral back down to Earth.

But when he opened his eyes, all he could see were stars shining in every direction as the rocket rushed silently through the inky blackness of space.

"We made it, Bonehead!" he exclaimed. "We're on the way to the moon!"

The only answer Snaffles received was the sound of munching!

Snaffles turned to see that Bonehead had woken up and taken off his space helmet. The dopey dog had his boots on the control panel and was happily tucking into a large sandwich.

"I don't believe it," Snaffles said, keeping his own helmet well and truly on his head. "Did you bring a packed lunch?"

"No boss," Bonehead replied, spraying buttered breadcrumbs everywhere. "I found this sarnie under my seat. Admiral Grumblechops must have left it there for me. I wonder how he knew I'd missed my tea?"

"Do you always think with your stomach?" the cat burglar asked, before taking a suspicious sniff. "What's in that sandwich anyway? It smells like–"

"Fish-paste," Bonehead interrupted happily, before something strange happened. A look of confusion passed over Bonehead's face. This in itself wasn't unusual. Bonehead was confused so often he could write a book about it. In fact, he started one once – '*How to be confused 25 hours a day*' by Bonehead the Bulldog. Unfortunately, he didn't get any further than writing the title before he was distracted by the thought of biscuits. To be fair that happens to a lot of writers. In fact, I really fancy a custard cream right now. Or maybe a jammy dodger.

What? I haven't time to go to the biscuit barrel because you want to know what happens next? Tsk. You lot are so demanding.

But if you *must* know, Bonehead's eyes started to spin like a nuclear-powered washing machine. The half-eaten sandwich dropped from his grasp.

"Is anything wrong, Bonehead, old boy," Snaffles queried nervously.

"Wroooooong," the zombified sidekick repeated before his eyes stopped spinning and instead glowed bright red!

"The fish-paste sandwich!" Snaffles realized. "It must have been planted by Moonfish! He's controlling what little mind you have through the contents of your snack!"

Bonehead snarled at Snaffles. The snarl turned into a growl and the growl turned into a bark. It wouldn't be long before the bark turned into a bite!

Snaffles fumbled with his seat belt, but his bulky astronaut gloves made it impossible to get free. The mind-controlled mutt leapt forward, teeth bared. Snaffles spun around and Bonehead's teeth sank deep into the chair back.

Finally pulling his seat belt apart, Snaffles floated weightlessly in the zero gravity. Behind him, Bonehead had already chomped through the chair and was glaring at his boss with hungry red eyes.

"Bonehead, wait! Snaffles cried, but it was too late. The dog lunged forward and grabbed Snaffles. The two former friends tumbled through the air, bouncing off walls and thudding into computers in the cramped cockpit.

"Stop it," Snaffles shouted as he crashed into the ceiling. "We'll hit something important in a minute!"

Thinking quickly, Snaffles grabbed Bonehead's helmet and slammed it back on to the crazed canine's head.

"Maybe that will block Moonfish's signal," he gasped.

Bonehead shook his head as if in a daze – and then resumed his attack!

"Or maybe not!" Snaffles said, as they spun towards the control panel and a large red button. Above the button was an even larger sign that read:

DO NOT CLICK THIS BUTTON!

(AND THAT MEANS YOU, BONEHEAD!)

LOVE ADMIRAL GRANDCHOPS
XX

Bonehead's knee collided with the button.

CLICK!

"*Self-destruct system initiated!*" announced a computerized voice. "*This rocket will be destroyed in approximately one second!*"

"Whaaat?" screamed Snaffles. "Surely you need to give us more warning than–"

BOOOOOOOOOOOOOOM!

Chapter 6

Moon Base Mayhem

If taking off in the rocket had been bad, having it blow up around them was even worse. A huge explosion ripped the spaceship apart, sending Snaffles spinning out into space.

Safe within his suit, the cat burglar shook his head, his ears still ringing. His paw went to the suit's controls and he opened a communication channel. "Bonehead, where are you? Please tell me the blast knocked some sense into you!"

"*Eat you!*" came the response. Snaffles looked up to see one of the rocket's boosters floating past Bonehead. The dog scrambled on to its back, pointing the booster at Snaffles. He was going to fly straight into him!

Glancing up at the moon, Snaffles had an idea. What had he said earlier? Bonehead always thought with his stomach! Of course!

"Bonehead, old pal," Snaffles said quickly into his radio communicator. "How was that sandwich? Nice and tasty?"

On the back of the booster, Bonehead tried to scratch his neck through his helmet. "*Urrrrrr…*"

"I bet there are a lot more sandwiches on the moon. Delicious, scrummy sandwiches with all kinds of fillings.

Fish-paste sandwiches… sausage sandwiches…" Snaffles decided to try Bonehead's favourite filling of all, "… even *bone* sandwiches!"

That did it. Bonehead's red eyes went wide and he licked his lips.

"*Eat sandwiches!*" he muttered, the thought of food breaking through Moonfish's control. Slamming his fist into the booster's controls, Bonehead fired the rocket. Whoooosh! It zoomed off at an angle, heading straight for the moon.

"That's my boy," Snaffles said, grabbing a cable from the wreckage and lassoing the hungry hound as he zipped by.

They pelted towards the dark side of the moon. Ahead of them, Snaffles saw a large moon base in the middle of a crater. It was round, like an upside-down goldfish bowl, and getting bigger every second.

They were going to crash into it!

"I say, old bean, time to slow down," Snaffles said, but the bulldog sped up. "You're going too fast. We're going to–"

CRASH!

The booster ploughed through the glass roof of the moon base and Snaffles and Bonehead smashed into a cold metal floor.

"Ugh!" Bonehead groaned. "What hit me?"

"Bonehead!" Snaffles cried out, jumping up to his feet. The fact that he didn't float into the air meant the moon base had artificial gravity. "You've come back to me!"

"Don't be silly, boss, I've not been anywhere," said Bonehead. "Er, where exactly are we anyway?"

Snaffles looked up at the ceiling. The hole they'd made was already repairing itself. Clever old moon base.

"We're a long way from home, Bonehead, that's where."

"And in t-t-t-trouble too, by the looks of it," Bonehead whined, pointing behind them.

Snaffles whirled around to see three large robots hovering towards them. They looked like giant silver cuttlefish, complete with writhing metal feelers in front of their mechanical eyes. If that wasn't bad enough, each and every feeler was topped by a vicious-looking laser cannon.

"STOP OR BE FILLETED!" the lead cuttlefish robot bellowed. To prove its point, a yellow laser beam screamed towards Snaffles. The cat burglar ducked and the laser bolt slammed harmlessly into a wall behind him.

"Quick, Bonehead, run!"

"You don't have to tell me twice," Bonehead said, before looking even more puzzled than usual. "Er, what is it we have to do again, boss?"

The other two robots fired lasers.

"RUN!" cried Snaffles.

Struggling to skedaddle in their oversized spacesuits, Snaffles and Bonehead charged beneath an arch and headed down a brightly-lit corridor. The entire place reeked of fish.

Behind them, the cyber-cuttlefish gave chase, laser cannons blazing.

"Quick, through here!" Snaffles said, yanking Bonehead towards a set of double-doors. The doors slid open, but Snaffles and Bonehead couldn't get far.

"Look out," Snaffles screeched, as they skidded to a halt. They were teetering on the edge of a gaping chasm. There was a door on the other side, but when they looked down, the yawning gap was so deep that they couldn't even see the bottom. It looked as if it went down to the centre of the moon!

"We can't go back," Snaffles said, punching a control with his tail. Behind them, the doors slid shut in the cuttlefishes' furious faces.

"That won't keep those r-r-robots out for long," Bonehead whimpered. Metallic feelers were already scraping against the doors.

"You're right for once, old chum," Snaffles agreed. "Whatever we're going to do, we need to do it quick!"

Chapter 7

A Prickly Problem

Behind Snaffles and Bonehead, a red dot appeared on the metal doors, smoke curling up from its centre.

"B-boss, the cyber-cuttlefishes," Bonehead jibbered. "They're b-burning through! I could b-bite them if you want?"

Snaffles could see that the bulldog was just trying to put a brave face on it, when in fact he was scared out of his wits – or rather he would be if he had any wits in the first place!

"Not to worry, old fruit," Snaffles said, concocting a plan. "I reckon we could swing across to the other side. "Look, there's a hook up there. If we knot our spacesuits together, we could make a rope!"

"And go where?" Bonehead bleated.

Snaffles glanced across the chasm. "To those doors, of...."

The cat burglar's voice trailed off as he saw the doors on the other side of the gap begin to open. Something popped out. Something that made Snaffles' mouth drop open.

"Ruffle my fur," Snaffles exclaimed. "It's some kind of... giant baby!"

Sure enough, the cutest robot fish you'd ever seen bobbed in the air in front of them.

If you can't quite imagine exactly how cute the fish actually was, here's a clue.

Take an adorable kitten and times it by a super-sweet puppy. Then, add a cuddly rabbit and multiply the whole lot with an angelic baby seal. That's only half as lovable as this robot fish. It had glistening scales and big black eyes and a delightful little mouth that turned up at the corners.

"Awwwwww," said Bonehead, completely forgetting about the cyber-cuttlefish that were making short work of the door. "What a little sweetie. And for a moment, I was worried that it would be something to hurt us." He waved coyly at the floating fish and said in a baby voice: "Who's a lovely likkle fishy-kins, then?"

The lovely likkle fishy-kins waved its lovely likkle fishy-kins tail in reply… and then did three things that could never, ever be described as lovely or indeed likkle.

1. It swelled to twice its original size, ballooning like a, well, a balloon, but one with gills and fins.

2. Spikes popped out all around its body. Sharp spikes. The kind of spikes you would never want to have fired at you across a bottomless chasm.

3. Just to complete the set, it started to fire its spikes at Snaffles and Bonehead across the bottomless chasm.

"Look out," Bonehead squealed, turning around and ducking to protect his head from the pointy projectiles.

"Yow!" the dog added loudly, as the very same projectiles planted themselves firmly in his rather plump rear.

"It's some kind of robot pufferfish," Snaffles realized, leaping around the narrow ledge to avoid the shooting spines.

"Ouch!" Bonehead yelled as more quivering quills buried themselves in his already throbbing backside. "Make it stop!"

"Yes, yes, there's no need to shout," Snaffles snapped as the deadly darts whistled past his whiskers. "I get your point!"

"Is that supposed to be funny?" Bonehead barked, his poor posterior looking more like a pincushion every second!

Using Bonehead's bottom as a shield, Snaffles shouted across to the fish. "Is that the best you can do, you balloon-faced loon?"

The pufferfish glowered, its body blowing up bigger than before. It was huge and its spines looked sharper than ever.

"What are you doing?" Bonehead wailed. "You're just making it angry!"

"Exactly," Snaffles agreed, still jeering at their outraged assailant. "And why not? It's not as if it can do anything, the over-blown gas-bag!"

The pufferfish was now so large that it wasn't even floating, but bounced up and down angrily on the platform across from them.

"Oooooh, look at me," Snaffles teased, blowing out his cheeks to mimic the robot. "I'm a big, bad pufferfish! Well, if you're so spiky, why don't you just roll over here and squash us?"

"Boss!" Bonehead squealed. "I thought I was supposed to be the stupid one. Be quiet will you?"

But the pufferfish had heard enough insults. To prove a point – no pun intended – it did exactly what the cat burglar had suggested. Snarling, the perfectly round robot rolled forwards, forgetting the colossal chasm that separated it from its prey. With a surprised gasp, it tumbled into the divide and stuck fast, bridging the gap.

"That's what I was waiting for," cheered Snaffles, leaping onto the back of the wedged pufferfish and sprinting to the other side. "Come on Bonehead, and watch out for those spikes!"

"Ow, ow, ow, ow!" said Bonehead as he scampered after the cat burglar and somehow managed to step on every spine in his way. He made it across just in time to see the cuttlefish finally smash their way through the door.

"HALT!" they commanded, hovering over the pufferfish's back.

"I don't think so," Snaffles smiled, yanking a spike from Bonehead's bottom. He plunged it into the side of the pufferfish. "It's a long way down, chaps!"

BANG!

The pufferfish burst like a metal bubble, sending the cyber-cuttlefish tumbling into the gloomy shaft below, robotic feelers flailing.

Snaffles threw the spike after them for good measure. "Ha! I didn't think they would fall for that one!"

Chapter 8

Don't Chute!

Bonehead took one last look at the plummeting pufferfish, then turned to his boss.

"What do we do now?" he asked, pulling the last barb from his bruised behind.

"Well, we can't go back," Snaffles said, leaping through the door ahead of them. "So I think it's a case of best paw forwa-aaaaaargh!"

When jumping through a door, it's always wise to check there is a floor on the other side. As advice goes, it's right up there with *never fall out of a plane without a parachute and it's best not to pop your head in a tiger's mouth.* Such was Snaffle's excitement that he completely forgot to look before he leapt and so found himself sliding down a particularly slippery garbage chute.

Even worse, he soon realized that Bonehead was sliding down above him.

He could tell this mainly because the dog was shouting: "Look out beloooooooooooooooooooooooooooooow!"

With a thud, Snaffles flew out of the bottom of the chute and landed on a huge heap of rubbish.

With an even bigger thud, Bonehead flew out of the bottom of the chute and landed on top of Snaffles.

"That was fun," giggled Bonehead.

"Not from where I'm sitting," Snaffles said, pushing the podgy pooch off his head. "But shush, can you hear something?"

"Yes!" nodded Bonehead.

"What is it?" asked Snaffles.

"It's you saying 'shush'," replied Bonehead.

"No, you befuddled bow-wow, I mean another voice!"

Snaffles scrambled over the pile of trash towards a vent in the wall. Yes! There was a voice, coming from the other side. Snaffles popped a claw and carefully unscrewed the vent, lifting it to the side. He popped his head through and peered down into the room below.

Sitting in front of a bank of computers was what looked like a goldfish in a goldfish bowl. But this wasn't an ordinary goldfish bowl. Oh no! This one had gangly robot arms and legs.

As Snaffles watched, the goldfish threw levers and pressed controls, all the time bellowing commands into a microphone that it wore strapped to the side of its head.

"Cyber-cuttlefish, find the intruders! Find them now!"

"Hey, boss," shouted Bonehead. "I recognize that voice! It's Moonfish!"

"Shhhh!" hissed Snaffles, but it was too late. Down in the control room, the goldfish bowl span around, it's tiny occupant spying them with beady eyes.

"There they are!" Moonfish screamed. "Guards! Get them!"

"Time to beat a retreat!" Snaffles suggested, but as they crawled back across the room, three more cyber-cuttlefish appeared from the garbage chute.

There was nowhere to hide!

"Don't worry, boss, I'll save you!" shouted Bonehead, snatching up Snaffles and barrelling through the vent.

"What are you doing!" the cat burglar cried as they dropped down into the control chamber, straight into Moonfish's mechanical clutches. The maniacally giggling goldfish snatched at them with whirring robot pincers before holding his prisoners at arm's length.

"So, this is the great Sniffles and his faithful hound, Binhead," Moonfish sneered from within his bowl, water slopping over its edge. Now that they were closer, Snaffles could see that an old scar stretched down the side of Moonfish's face, running right through a glassy left eye. "I have to say I'm rather disappointed by your performance."

"Tell me about it," Snaffles sniffed dismissively. "I thought we were chasing down a dangerous super-criminal, not a jumped-up sprat in an old goldfish bowl!"

"Yeah," agreed Bonehead. "And what's a goldfish doing on the moon anyway? It doesn't make much sense, if you ask me!"

"To be fair, nothing makes sense to you, Bonehead old buddy!" pointed out Snaffles, helpfully.

"That's true," Bonehead agreed, scratching the back of his neck.

"Are you two fools quite finished?" interrupted Moonfish. "Over 50 years I've been stuck on this worthless rock! Over half a century of planning my revenge! And the best the Earth can send is a pair of babbling, bird-brained nincompoops! You haven't even asked me the most important question yet!"

"Oh yes? And what question is that, you scaly squirt?" enquired Snaffles.

An evil smirk spread across Moonfish's orange features. "How am I going to destroy Snaffles the Cat Burglar once and for all?"

Chapter 9

Moonfish's Masterplan

Snaffles struggled in Moonfish's mechanical grasp, but couldn't twist free. Beside him, Bonehead was in the same boat, unable to move as Moonfish clomped across the control room.

"Bonehead, old chap," Snaffles whispered to his sidekick. "Moonfish has got tight hold of my spacesuit, but maybe I can wriggle out of the neck hole! Try to distract him, can you?"

"How?" Bonehead asked.

"Do I have to think of everything?"

Snaffles snapped back, despairing.

"Yes," Bonehead admitted.

"OK, then," Snaffles sighed. "Ask the scaly so-and-so a question!"

Nodding, Bonehead turned to their captor. "There's one thing I don't understand, Mr Moonfish, sir," he said.

"Only one?" Moonfish teased. "I find that hard to believe!"

"How on Earth did a goldfish end up on the moon?" Bonehead asked, completely missing the insult.

"A surprisingly intelligent question," Moonfish acknowledged. "I was blasted here as part of the Russian Space Programme, back in the 1950s."

"Why would the Russians send a fish into space?" Snaffles enquired, continuing his secret escape bid.

"They launched loads of animals into space," Moonfish explained, "Dogs, rabbits, monkeys and fish. The list went on and on."

"But why?" asked Bonehead.

"To check that space travel was safe for humans," came the bitter reply. "They didn't care what happened to us!"

"And you never got back to Earth?"

Moonfish shook his scarred head. "Something went wrong with my rocket. I crashed into the moon's surface."

"I know how that feels," Bonehead sympathized, rubbing his still-aching head.

"But my journey into space changed me forever!" continued Moonfish. "I was bombarded by cosmic rays that transformed me from a simple goldfish into a super-smart genius.

Constructing this base and its contents from the wreckage of my spaceship was child's play!"

"And all the time you plotted against the human race," Snaffles said. "Planning your revenge!"

"They left me to flounder in space," Moonfish hissed. "So I'll do the same to them, using *this*!"

Moonfish stopped beside a bank of computers. In front of them, a small device hung from the ceiling. it was like a helmet but covered in wires and flashing lights.

"Behold," Moonfish shrieked. "The mind-control-a-tron. This is my greatest invention."

"What does that do then?" Bonehead asked, innocently.

"What do you think it does, you dim-witted dog?" Moonfish growled. "The clue's in the name!"

"That's how you've been controlling the world's fish," Snaffles realized, both his arms and legs now free inside the suit.

"It certainly is!" crowed Moonfish, triumphantly. "And today they will rise from the seas to conquer every nation on Earth."

Pictures appeared on the computer screens, showing thousands of red-eyed fish waiting patiently beneath the waves. Each sat in a walking machine like Moonfish's own, with tiny bowls for tiddlers and huge tanks for humpback whales!

Humanity didn't stand a chance.

Inside his suit, Snaffles curled his tail into a spring, ready for action. "And what happens after you've conquered the Earth?"

Moonfish smiled evilly. "Every human on the planet will be loaded into rockets and fired into space, just as they did to me! Let's see how they like it!"

Snaffles had heard enough. "Sorry, old sprat," the cat burglar said, leaping through his spacesuit's neck hole, "but that plan sounds decidedly fishy to me!"

"Yay, boss!" Bonehead cheered as Snaffles span towards the mind-control-a-tron. The cat burglar already knew exactly what he was going to do. While Moonfish had ranted, Snaffles had worked out a full-proof plan. It ran like this:

SNAFFLES' FOOLPROOF PLAN TO SAVE THE DAY

Step one: Grab the mind-control-a-tron!

Step two: Slap the mind-control-a-tron onto my head.

Step three: Order the mind-controlled fish on Earth to turn on each other.

Step four: Make a clever pun to show how brilliant I am. Something funny like: "That should stop you carping on!" or "I've haddock enough of you!"

Step five: Grab Moonfish.

Step six: Deliver the fiend back to Earth and collect a ginormous reward, or maybe a nice shiny medal. Hopefully both.

It was a great plan. One of Snaffles' best. Nothing could go wrong – until the cat burglar wondered just how shiny his shiny medal would be.

Snaffles had always loved shiny things, ever since he'd stolen a solid diamond baby's dummy as a kitten. Now, flying through the air, he let his mind wander. He was so distracted by the thought of his medal that he didn't spot a cyber-cuttlefish blocking his path and–

SLAM!

Snaffles smacked headfirst into the robot guard.

"Boo, boss!" Bonehead groaned, as Snaffles became tangled in the cuttlefish's terrible tentacles.

"Ha-ha-ha-haaaaa," giggled Moonfish. "You'll have to try harder than that if you want to foil my plans – not that you'll have the oppor-*tuna*-ty!"

Below them, a trapdoor slid open to reveal a deep pit. At the bottom, lurked a giant gleaming oyster. The menacing mollusc opened its steel shell as Snaffles was dragged to the edge of the pit.

"Boss," Bonehead yelled helplessly. "They're going to throw you to that barnacled beast!"

"Yes, thank you, Bonehead," Snaffles shouted as he was tossed towards the oyster's open mouth. "I'd worked that out for myseeeeeeeeeeeelf!"

CLACK!

Chapter 10

The Big Fin-ish

The clam's shell snapped together around Snaffles. Desperately, the cat burglar pushed against the oyster's sides, trying to prise the monstrous mollusc open again. It wouldn't budge. Snaffles was trapped!

Above the pit, the mind-control-a-tron dropped onto Moonfish's golden head.

"This is it, my watery warriors," he announced, his thoughts transmitted thousands of miles across space. "Prepare to take your *plaice* as the new masters of Earth!"

"The boss will stop you," Bonehead barked, still held tight in Moonfish's robotic grip. "Just you wait and sea… er, I mean see!"

"I don't think so, Binhead," Moonfish gloated. "Soon the world will be my oyster!"

Of course, Snaffles couldn't hear any of this. He was too busy trying to escape his own oyster!

It can't end like this, he thought, wracking his cat burglar brain to think of a way out. *Think of all the gold, jewels and pearls I've yet to pinch!*

"That's it!" he exclaimed out loud, an idea striking him like a frying pan to the back of his head. "Pearls!"

Snaffles knew everything there was to know about pearls. They were one of his favourite subjects — after himself, of course.

"Pearls come from oysters," he remembered, "forming when they're irritated by pesky parasites trapped inside their shells."

Snaffles started tickling the inside of the colossal clam's shell. Immediately, the oyster started to shake.

"I doubt this thing can make pearls, but I can definitely make it very uncomfortable!"

The more Snaffles tickled, the more the oyster trembled. It shook and convulsed, trying to stop itself from sniggering, until it could take no more. Without warning, the oyster opened its shell and let out the biggest belly laugh you've ever heard.

"HA!"

The laugh was just the beginning of a series of incredible events that went like this:

1. The chuckling clam spat Snaffles straight out of the pit. Whoosh!
2. He barrelled into Bonehead, who in turn barged into Moonfish's goldfish bowl. Crash!
3. The glass shattered, sending water splashing everywhere. Splosh!
4. Moonfish shrieked and fell to the floor. Splat!
5. The mind-control-a-thon swung on its cord before fixing itself firmly onto Bonehead's forehead! Plop!

"What's happening?" wailed Bonehead, but Snaffles just grinned.

His *second* foolproof plan was working purr-fectly!

As soon as the cap settled on Bonehead's bonce, the mind-control-a-thon transmitted the canine's confusion straight to Earth's oceans.

All at once, every sea creature that had been under Moonfish's control scratched the backs of their necks. Even the jellyfish, who don't really have necks at all!

A minute ago they'd all been ready to take over the world. Now, they were completely befuddled by Bonehead's bewildered brainwaves!

Back on the moon, the mind-control-a-thon sparked and crackled.

"The machine can't cope with your confusion, Bonehead old buddy," Snaffles said, giving his sidekick a friendly shove out of the way. "It's going to overload! RUN!"

Sure enough, as soon as Bonehead was clear, the mind-control-a-tron exploded with a big, satisfying BANG!

All around them, the cyber-cuttlefish charged this way and that, their circuits completely fried by the explosion. Tentacles writhing, they crashed into each other before collapsing in a heap.

Wasting no time, Snaffles jumped to his feet and looked around.

"Bonehead, where's Moonfish?"

The bulldog pointed towards the computer screens that now showed a small rocket taking off outside the moonbase. As they watched, the picture switched to Moonfish's flushed face, glaring down at them.

"*You may have defeated me this time, Snuffles, but this is one fish that got away,*" the ghastly goldfish gloated from the safety of his escape capsule. "*I'll be back, have no* trout! *Moonfish will return!*"

"And I'll be waiting," Snaffles promised, as the screens went black.

"So, is it all over?" Bonehead asked, scratching his neck.

"For now, my faithful friend," Snaffles said, slapping Bonehead on the back. "Moonfish may have skedaddled, but the Earth is safe. Let's call Admiral Grandchops and have the old walrus send a rocket to take us home!"

"*Fin*-tastic," Bonehead beamed. "I know exactly what I'm going to cook for a celebratory meal when we get back!"

"What's that, old boy?"

"Fish surprise!" Bulldog said proudly.

"Hmmmm, maybe not, old fruit," Snaffles said with a sly smile. "I think I've had quite enough of those!"

THE END

FICTION EXPRESS

THE READERS TAKE CONTROL!

Have you ever wanted to change the course of a plot, change a character's destiny, tell an author what to write next?

Well, now you can!

'Snaffles and the Moonfish Mystery' was originally written for the award-winning interactive e-book website Fiction Express.

Fiction Express e-books are published in gripping weekly episodes. At the end of each episode, readers are given voting options to decide where the plot goes next. They vote online and the winning vote is then conveyed to the author who writes the next episode, in real time, according to the readers' most popular choice.

www.fictionexpress.co.uk

WINNER
Education Resources
Award for Innovation

FICTION EXPRESS

TALK TO THE AUTHORS

The Fiction Express website features a blog where readers can interact with the authors while they are writing. An exciting and unique opportunity!

FANTASTIC TEACHER RESOURCES

Each weekly Fiction Express episode comes with a PDF of teacher resources packed with ideas to extend the text.

"The teaching resources are fab and easily fill a whole week of literacy lessons!"
Rachel Humphries, teacher at Westacre Middle School

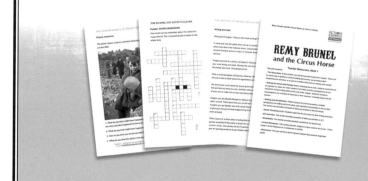

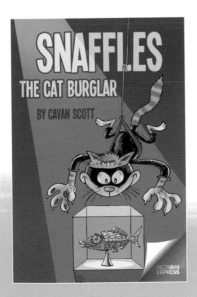

FICTI🗩N EXPRESS

Rise of the Rabbits
by Barry Hutchison

When twins Harvey and Lola are given the school rabbit, Mr Lugs, to look after for the weekend, they're both very excited. That is until the rabbit begins to mutate and decides the time has come for bunnies to rise up and seize control.

It's up to Harvey and Lola to find a way to return Mr Lugs and his friends to normal, before the menaces sweep across the country – and then the world!

ISBN 978-1-78322-540-8

FICTI●N EXPRESS

The Sand Witch
by Tommy Donbavand

When twins Chris and Ella are left to look after their younger brother on a deserted beach, they expect everything to be normal, boring in fact. But then something extraordinary happens! Will the Sand Witch succeed in passing on her sandy curse in this exciting adventure?

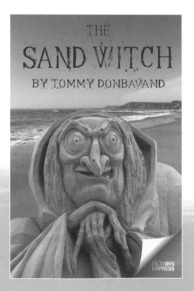

ISBN 978-1-78322-544-6

FICTI●N EXPRESS

The Vampire Quest
by Simon Cheshire

James is an ordinary boy, but his best friend Vince is a bit...
odd. For one thing, it turns out that Vince is a vampire. His
parents are vampires, too. And so are the people who live
at No. 38. There are vampires all over the place, it seems,
but there's nothing to worry about. They like humans, and
they'd never, ever do anything...horrible to them. Unless...
the world runs out of Feed-N-Gulp, the magical vegetarian
vampire brew. Which is exactly what's just happened....

ISBN 978-1-78322-553-8

About the Author

With over 90 books and audios to his name, No 1 bestselling author Cavan Scott has written *Star Wars*, *Doctor Who*, *The Penguins of Madagascar*, *Adventure Time*, *Danger Mouse* and *Skylanders*. He also writes *Minnie the Minx*, *Roger the Dodger*, *Bananaman* and more for the world famous Beano comic.

Cavan lives in Bristol with his wife, two daughters and an inflatable Dalek called Desmond. Check out his website at www.cavanscott.com